TRACKING THE DIPLODOCUS

DINOSAUR COVE™

TRACKING THE DIPLODOCUS

BY
REX STONE

ILLUSTRATED BY
MIKE SPOOR

SCHOLASTIC INC.

New York Toronto London Auckland
Sydney Mexico City New Delhi Hong Kong

SPECIAL THANKS TO JANE CLARKE
FOR ANDY AND ROB, WITH LOVE – R.S.
FOR MY HANNAH, AT LAST – M.S.

ISBN: 978-0-545-11247-5

Text copyright © 2010 by Working Partners Ltd. All rights reserved.
Illustrations copyright © 2010 by Mike Spoor.

Dinosaur Cove series created by Working Partners Ltd., London.
DINOSAUR COVE is a registered trademark of
Working Partners Ltd.

Published by Scholastic Inc., 557 Broadway,
New York, NY 10012, by arrangement with Working Partners Ltd.
SCHOLASTIC, LITTLE APPLE, and associated logos are trademarks
and/or registered trademarks of Scholastic Inc.

12 11 10 9 8 7 6 5 4 3 2 1   10 11 12 13 14 15/0

Printed in the U.S.A.   40
First printing, February 2010

FACT FILE

JAMIE AND HIS BEST FRIEND, TOM, HAVE DISCOVERED A SECRET CAVE WITH FOSSILIZED DINOSAUR FOOTPRINTS AND, WHEN THEY PLACE THEIR FEET OVER EACH OF THE FOSSILS IN TURN, THEY ARE MAGICALLY TRANSPORTED TO A WORLD WITH REAL, LIVE DINOSAURS. BUT THE BOYS NEVER IMAGINED THAT VISITING DINO WORLD WOULD BE JUST LIKE GOING TO THE DENTIST....

JAMIE

- FULL NAME: JAMIE MORGAN
- AGE: 8 YEARS
- SIZE: 1 JATOM*
- TOP SPEED: 7 MPH
- LIKES: FOSSIL HUNTING AND LEARNING ABOUT DINOSAURS
- DISLIKES: BEING STUCK INDOORS

Jamie's eye

Jamie's foot

Jamie's hand

*NOTE: A JATOM IS THE SIZE OF JAMIE OR TOM: 4 FT TALL AND 60 LBS IN WEIGHT.

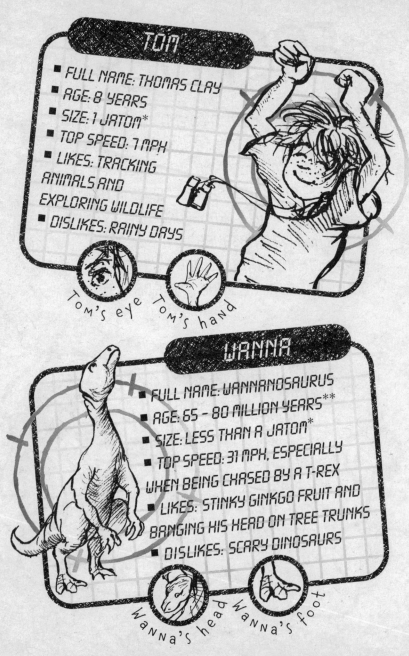

TOM

- FULL NAME: THOMAS CLAY
- AGE: 8 YEARS
- SIZE: 1 JATOM*
- TOP SPEED: 7 MPH
- LIKES: TRACKING ANIMALS AND EXPLORING WILDLIFE
- DISLIKES: RAINY DAYS

Tom's eye Tom's hand

WANNA

- FULL NAME: WANNANOSAURUS
- AGE: 65 – 80 MILLION YEARS**
- SIZE: LESS THAN A JATOM*
- TOP SPEED: 31 MPH, ESPECIALLY WHEN BEING CHASED BY A T-REX
- LIKES: STINKY GINKGO FRUIT AND BANGING HIS HEAD ON TREE TRUNKS
- DISLIKES: SCARY DINOSAURS

Wanna's head Wanna's foot

*NOTE: A JATOM IS THE SIZE OF JAMIE OR TOM: 4 FT TALL AND 60 LBS IN WEIGHT.
**NOTE: SCIENTISTS CALL THIS PERIOD THE LATE CRETACEOUS.

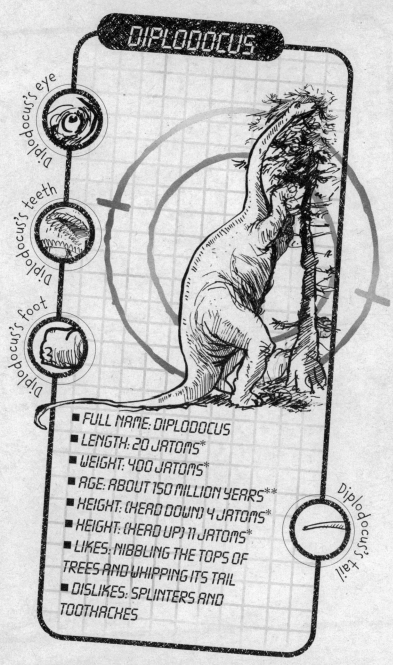

DIPLODOCUS

Diplodocus's eye

Diplodocus's teeth

Diplodocus's foot

Diplodocus's tail

- FULL NAME: DIPLODOCUS
- LENGTH: 20 JATOMS*
- WEIGHT: 400 JATOMS*
- AGE: ABOUT 150 MILLION YEARS**
- HEIGHT: (HEAD DOWN) 4 JATOMS*
- HEIGHT: (HEAD UP) 11 JATOMS*
- LIKES: NIBBLING THE TOPS OF TREES AND WHIPPING ITS TAIL
- DISLIKES: SPLINTERS AND TOOTHACHES

*NOTE: A JATOM IS THE SIZE OF JAMIE OR TOM: 4 FT TALL AND 60 LBS IN WEIGHT.
**NOTE: SCIENTISTS CALL THIS PERIOD THE JURASSIC.

"**W**here are you, Grandpa?" Jamie Morgan's voice echoed around the dinosaur museum on the ground floor of the lighthouse. "We're off to hunt for dinosaurs!"

"He'll think we mean fossil dinosaurs, not real ones," Tom Clay whispered. The two friends grinned at each other. Only they knew the amazing secret of Dinosaur Cove — a cave that led to a world of real, live dinosaurs!

"Grandpa?" Jamie called again. As he slung his backpack over his shoulders and stepped

into the lobby of the museum, his feet crunched on something gritty.

"Why are these seeds all over the floor?" Tom wondered. "Maybe he's gardening?"

They hurried out the front door and looked around the cliff top. There was no sign of Jamie's grandfather.

There was a flash of yellow as a little bird with a red head swooped down and began to peck at something on a flat rock beside a bush near the edge of the cliff.

"Look," Tom said, pointing to the trail of seeds that led to the rock where the bird was feasting. The branches of the bush rustled.

"Grandpa?" Jamie called, making the bird fly off.

"Shhhhh!" hissed the bush.

Jamie laughed in surprise as his grandfather's mop of unruly hair emerged from the leaves.

"What are you doing?" Jamie asked, running over.

"This is my bird hide," Jamie's grandfather whispered. "I'm taking part in a survey, recording all the different birds that visit Dinosaur Cove. That was a goldfinch."

"Sorry, we scared it away," Tom said.

"It'll come back for the birdseed." The captain's eyes twinkled. "It can't resist the bait. Why don't you boys try some bird-watching?"

"Awesome idea! We know just the place to do it." Jamie nudged Tom.

Jamie's grandfather held up his finger. "Remember, the secret of bird-watching is to stay quiet and hidden." He tapped his nose, then ducked back into the bush.

"See you later, Grandpa!" Jamie called.

They raced off along the path toward Smugglers' Point.

"Got the ammonite?" Tom asked.

Jamie patted his pocket. "The Jurassic one," he confirmed as they reached the cave. The spiral fossil was the key to which time period they would visit.

Jamie took out his flashlight, and they squeezed through the tiny gap at the back of the cave into the secret chamber that led to Dino World. His heart was thumping with excitement as he fitted his feet into the fossil footprints. He took a deep breath and stepped

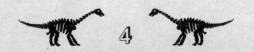

toward the cave wall. "One, two, three, four . . . FIVE!"

A crack of light appeared in the solid rock, and suddenly he was in the sweltering sunlight of Dino World. His ears filled with the sounds of insects buzzing and the strange

calls of unseen creatures out there in the Jurassic jungle.

There was a squelch as Tom stepped on the slimy pile of leaves beside him, stirring up a familiar smell in the hot, humid air.

"Phew!" Tom gagged. "The ginkgo fruit must be ripe. They're even stinkier than usual."

"Wanna will love them." Jamie made a face.

At the mention of his name, a little dinosaur with a bony head bounded up to the boys on his two back legs, wagging his tail and making happy grunting noises.

"He's pleased to see us." Tom laughed. "It's good to see you again, Wanna."

Wanna looked up hopefully at the fruit-laden ginkgo tree.

"I'll get you one." Jamie wrinkled his nose and reached out for an apricot-sized fruit on a nearby branch. It was so ripe that sticky ginkgo goo squished through his fingers.

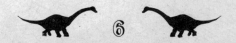

He tried to toss the fruit to the little dinosaur, but it stuck fast to his hand.

"Yuck!" Jamie held out his hand. Wanna slurped down the fruit, then licked the sticky juice off Jamie's fingers with his sandpaper tongue.

"Gross!" Jamie wiped the dino drool onto his jeans.

"Since Wanna
loves ginkgoes
so much,"
Tom said
thoughtfully,
"maybe we
should take
some along to bait
flying reptiles, like
birdseed."

"We'll be the very
first Jurassic bird-watchers."

Jamie filled a plastic bag
with the foul-smelling fruit and
stuffed it in his backpack. He held
out his hands for Wanna to clean.

"Let's go dino bird-watching!"

Tom and Jamie plunged into the steamy Jurassic jungle and began to wade through the sea of ferns beneath the tall trees. Wanna followed them closely, with his eyes firmly fixed on Jamie's backpack.

Tom looked up.

"What is it?" Jamie asked, pushing a fern out of his face.

"I can't see anything," Tom complained as another fern swayed back and forth in front of his face. "We need to find a gap in the jungle."

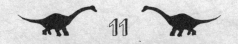

They pressed on through the thick undergrowth until they came to a clearing scattered with enormous flat rocks.

"This looks like a good place for bird-watching," Tom said. "Where shall we hide?"

Jamie looked around. "How about up there?" He pointed to a tall tree on the edge of the clearing. It was draped with thick, ropelike vines. Halfway up, two sturdy branches emerged from the trunk together, making a safe platform to sit on.

"Looks good," Tom agreed, "but the birds might see us."

"Not if we make a dino-bird hide!" Jamie said excitedly.

"Cool." Tom grinned. "Like a tree house."

"We can use ferns for the roof and sides. . . ." Jamie grabbed hold of the thick stem of a broadleaf fern and pulled with all his might. "I can't pull it up," he panted, "it's too tough."

As he spoke, the fern gave way with a sudden *pop* and he fell backward onto the soggy ground. He stood up covered in mud, with pine needles and bits of dead fern sticking to his clothes.

"I look like a swamp monster," he spluttered.

Splat!

Tom laughed. "But it's awesome camouflage. A bit more and you'll look like part of the jungle." He grabbed a handful of tender fern tips and stuffed them down the neck of Jamie's T-shirt.

"I'll get you for that!" Jamie scooped up an armful of soft mud and hurled it toward Tom.

Tom stepped sideways and the muck hit Wanna. *Splat!*

"Missed me!" Tom burst into laughter at the sight of the muck-covered dinosaur. Wanna didn't seem to like that. He wagged his tail and lowered his head.

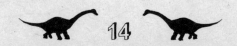

"Go, Wanna, go!" Jamie cheered as Wanna gently barged Tom into the muddy ooze. Jamie rushed over and stuffed some fern tips down his friend's neck.

"Now you're camouflaged, too!" Jamie said, laughing.

After a moment, Tom struggled to his feet. "We'll scare away the wildlife with all this noise. Let's get on with making the hide."

The boys both gathered an armful of dead leaves, then climbed the tree and began weaving them through the dangling vines to make the sides of the hide.

Down below, Wanna put his head on one side and watched curiously. Then he sighed deeply and curled up in the ferns.

"Wanna's taking a nap," Jamie whispered, peering down at the little dinosaur through a gap in the fern wall.

"That's good," Tom said, laying the last of the ferns across the top of the hide to make a roof. "Let's hope he stays still and quiet."

Jamie took out his notebook and wrote DINO BIRD SURVEY at the top of one page. Tom smiled, then they peered out through the fern wall into the clearing, watching and waiting.

After a few minutes, something flapped onto the branch above them.

Through a gap in the fern roof, Jamie could see the claws on the creature's feet gripping on to

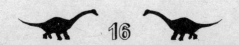

the branch. It looked like an overgrown woodpecker with electric blue feathers. "Archaeopteryx," he breathed.

"Awesome," Tom whispered. "Its beak's full of razor-sharp teeth."

As Jamie leaned closer, the fern tips sticking out of his T-shirt tickled his nose. "A . . . a . . . achoo!" He sneezed.

The archaeopteryx took off in an explosion of twigs. Something white and slimy splattered on the fern roof of the hide and dripped down, narrowly missing Jamie's shoulder.

"Yurgh!" Tom grimaced.
"Archaeopteryx poo!"

Jamie smiled and opened his notebook to the dino-bird survey page. He wrote ARCHAEOPTERYX 1 and sketched a picture of the bird. They had seen an archaeopteryx on an earlier adventure in Dino World. Jamie hoped the next entry would be something new and even more exciting.

"Let's put out some ginkgoes," Tom whispered, taking the plastic bag out of Jamie's backpack.

"Don't wake Wanna," Jamie warned him. "Or he'll eat them all."

As quietly as he could, Tom stretched up his arm and squished a ginkgo fruit onto a branch, sticking it down.

"Let's see what takes the bait," he whispered.

The boys sat, peering through the gaps in the ferns and waiting for the dino birds.

Nothing came. Jamie shifted uncomfortably on the branch. It was hard sitting still and waiting, but the boys were determined. Tom flipped open the Fossil Finder to pass the time. He typed in *JURASSIC FLYING REPTILES*. "My favorite flier's

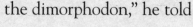

the dimorphodon," he told Jamie. "It has a beak like a puffin."

"Shh," Jamie whispered.

Just then, the branches of the tree rustled as a dark orange pterosaur with a wingspan as wide as Jamie's outstretched arms landed on the branch.

"Is it a dimorphodon?" Tom asked.

The creature scooped up a jawful of ginkgo fruit, dangling its long, thin tail with a kite-shape tip in front of their noses.

"No, that's a rhamphorhynchus," Jamie whispered excitedly, noting it on his dino-bird survey.

Tom looked closely at the flying reptile's long, thin jaws. "Its teeth crisscross," he said in surprise.

Jamie started to sketch the creature.

Thunk!

The tree trunk wobbled, and Jamie only just managed to hang on to his notebook. Beneath them, Wanna was standing back from the tree. He lowered his head and barged it into the trunk.

Thunk! The tree wobbled again. The rhamphorhynchus launched itself into the air with a squawk.

"Stop it, Wanna!" Tom called down. "You'll scare everything away." "He must be bored," Jamie said. "A few ginkgoes will keep him quiet." He dropped a stinky fruit, which splattered at Wanna's feet. But the little dinosaur took no notice. He head butted the tree again.

Thunk!

Tom and Jamie looked at each other.

"I don't believe it," Jamie gasped. "Wanna *never* ignores ginkgoes."

"Something's wrong," Tom said nervously.

The tree shook.

"That wasn't Wanna," Tom gulped. "Wanna's trying to warn us. Something's coming!"

CHAPTER 3

A humongous dappled green lizardy head burst through the front wall of their fern hide, tearing it clean away.

"Get down!" Jamie shouted as the creature swept off the flimsy roof and opened its toothy jaws.

The boys flattened themselves against the thick branch they were sitting on.

Scruuuuunch!

The tree shook as the long-necked dinosaur stripped the vines from the branch above them.

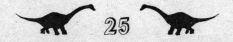

Tom gulped. "What is it?"

The gigantic beast grabbed hold of another branch and raked off the pine needles, chewing the greenery with its peg-like teeth.

Jamie heaved a huge sigh of relief. "It's a plant eater."

Tom grinned. "And with those nostrils on the top of its snout, it's got to be a diplodocus!" Jamie pulled out his Fossil Finder and looked up *DIPLODOCUS. IT EATS TONS OF VEGETATION A DAY TO FUEL ITS HUGE BODY, BUT DOESN'T STOP TO CHEW,* he read. *IT SWALLOWS STONES TO GRIND UP ITS FOOD.*

"Cool," Tom said. "It's an eating machine."

Jamie stashed the Fossil Finder and his notebook in his backpack as the diplodocus's nose swept away the rest of the fern hide. It sniffed deeply and moved toward Jamie. Its long neck and head were covered in giraffe-like markings in shades of jungle green.

"Keep still," Tom hissed. "It wants to eat your ferns, not you!"

The dinosaur's rubbery lips nuzzled at the fresh fern tips sticking out of the neck of Jamie's T-shirt.

"It tickles!" Jamie giggled as the lizardy lips nibbled at the leaves. Below them, Wanna had settled down, realizing that they weren't in danger.

Tom pulled the fern leaves out of his shirt and held them out on the palm of his hand. "Here you are."

The gigantic beast took them gently and gulped them down.

"It's like feeding a huge horse," Tom whispered.

The boys watched as the diplodocus stripped more branches of pine needles and swallowed some of the smaller twigs whole, leaving bare branches draped with dinosaur drool.

"This tree would make better dino toothpicks than lunch," Jamie commented.

"There are some younger vines and branches at the top, Dippy," Tom said. "Those would be tastier."

As if it'd heard, the huge dino reared up on its hind legs.

"Awesome!" Jamie murmured. They could see the diplodocus's pale yellow tummy as its elephantine front legs pawed the air and its long neck stretched out to grab the thickest branch at the top of the tree.

The branch bent, but instead of raking off the leaves and the vines, the dinosaur

hung on to it. The whole tree began to bend and shake.

"Dippy! Let go of the branch," Tom shouted, hugging the shuddering tree. There was a *craaack* as the branch broke off and a *thump* as the diplodocus's feet hit the earth. The tree swayed back and forth, but the boys managed to cling to their branch.

"Phew!" Jamie breathed. Beneath them, they could see Dippy con-tentedly chomping on the branch, breaking it into small pieces to gulp down. Suddenly, the dinosaur's eyes bulged and it swung its head up and began to shake it violently from side to side, making frantic sucking sounds with its tongue.

"What's happening now?" Tom looked worried.

"I'm not sure," Jamie replied, "but it doesn't look good."

The dinosaur's movements became even more erratic, and the boys worried about Wanna getting trampled on the ground.

"Dippy's freaking out!" Tom yelled. "Let's get out of here before it knocks us off."

But before they could scramble down the tree, Dippy started to bellow, rearing up on its hind legs and thrashing its front feet.

"Hang on," Jamie yelled as two huge dinosaur feet flailed at the tree.

The tree bent and sprang back, catapulting Tom off the branch. Jamie watched helplessly as his friend fell, clawing wildly at the air.

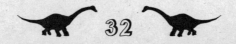

Luckily, he landed on the diplodocus's neck, wrapping his arms around it to stop himself from falling farther.

"I meant hang on to the tree, not the dinosaur!" Jamie yelled as the huge dinosaur stomped into the jungle with Tom swinging from its long, swaying neck.

CHAPTER 4

From his tree, Jamie could see Dippy shaking its head wildly from side to side. Any minute now, Tom would fall off or be crushed against a tree trunk. He had to save his friend!

The end of a thick vine dangled before him. Jamie took a deep breath, grabbed on to the vine, and launched himself toward the next tree. He swung safely across to a thick branch with more vines hanging down. He took hold and leaped off, swinging from tree to tree through the jungle after Tom.

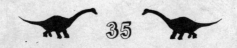

Beneath him,
Wanna was jumping
over logs and dodging
branches in his
struggle to keep up.
"Yee-haw!"
Jamie called as he
swung, and soon
he was alongside the
lumbering diplodocus.
Tom had slipped
under the dinosaur's

Help!

neck, just below
its head, and was
clinging on for
dear life.
"Help!" Tom
shouted at the top
of his lungs. "I
can't hold on
much longer!"

"I'll get you," Jamie shouted
back. He launched himself onto another vine
and swung across Dippy's path. "Grab my
hand!"

The boys' fingertips brushed as Jamie swung
past the dinosaur's eyes, but he wasn't close
enough to reach Tom.

Dippy stopped thrashing its head and
looked in amazement as Jamie swung back
onto the tree.

"I'm coming again." Jamie took a deep breath and launched himself from the same vine. He swung toward Tom, rising higher and higher, right above the dino's head! At the top of the swing, he stretched his hand down to Tom. Tom reached up, and they interlocked their fingers.

Jamie had him!

Snap! The vine gave way.

Jamie plummeted down, and was only saved by his friend's firm grip. While Tom held on to Dippy's neck with all his might, Jamie pulled himself up toward the giant reptile's scaly head and clawed for a handhold. He grabbed what felt like a slimy rubbery ledge. He was dangling from Dippy's spitty bottom lip.

Whoooooooo!

Dippy dropped its head and Jamie quickly let go and tumbled to the ground. Tom landed in a heap beside him.

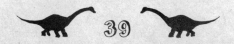

As Dippy pulled away, Jamie could see a piece of wood the size of a baseball bat lodged between the dinosaur's brown teeth and rubbery green gums.

"That was awesome!" Tom gasped. "I've never swung from a dinosaur before."

"First time for me, too," Jamie panted, trying to catch his breath as he untangled himself from his backpack.

Wanna hurtled out of the jungle and leaped on them, grunting enthusiastically.

grunk!
grunk!
grunk!

"Get off, we're OK!" Jamie struggled to his feet.

Whoooooo!

Dippy was wailing again, scraping its jaws along the ground. Then it lifted its head and shook it from side to side.

"I know what's making it so crazy," Jamie told Tom. "I saw a splinter of branch stuck between its teeth."

As they watched the huge dinosaur stomp off again, Tom said, "Poor Dippy's got a toothache."

Jamie nodded. "I had a toothache once and it really hurt."

"We need a dinosaur dentist," Tom said, "but we can't just call one up."

The boys looked at each other and grinned.

"Let's go after it," Jamie said.

Tom nodded. "*We'll* be Dippy's dentists!"

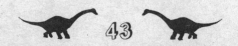

43

CHAPTER 5

SEARCH:

"**F**ollow Dippy!" Tom set off in the direction of a series of circular dents in the jungle floor.

Wanna dashed ahead and stopped at a mound of slimy orange mush, bobbing his head up and down.

"Good thing Dippy's left a clear trail," Jamie commented.

"He's squashed ferns, too." Tom pointed out a heap of crushed fronds.

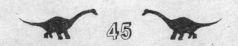

Something wet and slimy splattered down Jamie's neck. Slimy strings of frothy saliva were dripping from the tree Dippy had been walking under.

"Dino drool," he told Tom. "Dippy must have scraped its mouth against the branch to try and get that splinter out of its jaw."

The trail led them to a part of the jungle crisscrossed with pathways and dinosaur footprints.

"Other diplodocuses are using these paths," Jamie said in dismay. "I can't make out Dippy's trail."

The boys scanned the jungle.

"I think it went this way." Tom set off along a well-treaded jungle path, but Wanna grabbed his sleeve and dug his heels into the ground.

Jamie laughed. "I think Wanna thinks you're going the wrong way."

Wanna let go of Tom and then set off down another pathway.

The boys chased after Wanna and soon burst into a clearing scattered with enormous flat rocks.

"We're back where we started!" Jamie exclaimed. "We've gone around in a circle."

"There's Dippy." Tom pointed to the far side of the rocks. "It looks exhausted."

The huge dinosaur was dragging its enormous feet and staggering. As they watched, Dippy's legs buckled and it fell with a humongous

CRASH!

The earth shuddered beneath Tom's and Jamie's feet, and there was a moment's silence in the jungle before the insects resumed their relentless buzzing.

Dippy lay on its side, with its long neck and tail stretched out.

"Oh, no," Jamie said. "Is it dead?"

"No," Tom replied. "Its rib cage is moving and there's froth bubbling

from its mouth. It's just exhausted. We can still help."

They hurried toward the collapsed dinosaur. Its beady eyes looked at them, but it didn't move. Oily tears oozed from Dippy's eyes. It opened its mouth with a pitiful low *whoooooooooo*.

"We've got to get that splinter out," Tom said. "If it's too exhausted to move, the Jurassic scavengers will get it."

"A real dentist would get it out in no time," Jamie said.

"It'd never fit in a dentist's chair!" Tom joked.

Jamie and Tom lay on their tummies and wriggled up to the dinosaur's mouth. A blast of warm dino breath and frothy saliva hit them full in the face.

"Yuck!" Jamie gagged. "Its breath smells like rotten eggs."

"I can't see the splinter," Tom said, wiping the froth away from Dippy's jaws. "We need to get rid of some of this spit."

Jamie helped, and soon the boys could see Dippy's teeth, like two rows of brown tent pegs set in rubbery green gums. The splinter was stuck in its gum between two back teeth.

"I think I can get it out." Jamie gently reached his arm inside the dinosaur's mouth and grabbed the end of the splinter. Dippy's mouth felt warm and slimy.

Whooooooooo.

The gigantic beast moaned but kept still.

"Careful," Tom breathed.

"Open wide, Dippy." Jamie tugged at the splinter, but his hands only slipped down the wood.

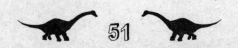

"Do real dentists get covered in this much spit?" Jamie groaned. "I can't get a good grip."

"Let me try," Tom told him.

Jamie wriggled to one side and wiped the dino drool on his jeans while Tom reached in.

"It's much too slimy," Tom agreed.

Dippy closed his eyes as the boys sat back on their heels.

"We're not helping; we're just hurting it more," Tom said with a frown.

Above them came the sound of flapping wings. Dark gray shapes began to circle like vultures above the exhausted diplodocus.

"Pterodactyls." Jamie leaped to his feet and shook his fists at them. "Go away!" he yelled.

Wanna took one look at them and dashed into the jungle.

The sharp-beaked pterodactyls flapped onto

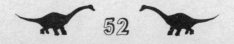

the branch of a nearby tree and sat there, hunched and waiting.

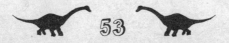

CHAPTER 6

Wanna crept back into the clearing with a mouthful of soft, juicy ferns, and put them straight into Dippy's mouth.

Dippy halfheartedly spat them out.

"It's a good idea to feed it." Tom patted Wanna's head. "But it's in too much pain to eat."

"It'll die if we give up on it," Jamie said, glancing up at the pterodactyls. "We have to keep trying. How can we get a better grip on that splinter?"

Wanna began hopping from foot to foot, grunting hopefully.

"He wants a ginkgo," Tom said. "You'd better give him one or he'll never let us get on with it."

Jamie got out the plastic bag. All the remaining ginkgo fruit was squashed together in a stinky, sticky mess.

"Yuck!" He opened the bag and laid it on the ground in front of Wanna. Wanna sniffed at the bag but didn't make a move to eat the ginkgoes; he just looked at Jamie, panting.

Jamie tried to wipe off the foul-smelling juice on his T-shirt, but it was stuck fast to his hands.

"That's what Wanna was trying to tell us," Jamie said. "We can use ginkgo glue!" He took another handful of mushy ginkgoes out of the bag and wriggled on his tummy up to Dippy's jaws.

Tom grabbed a handful of ginkgo pulp as well and crawled over to help.

Jamie gently mashed the gooey ginkgoes along the splinter of wood. "It's sticking!"

Tom knelt beside Jamie. "I'll grab on, too."

Together they started pulling. "It's moving," Jamie said. There was a sucking, squelching sound, then the boys fell backward as the splinter came free.

Whooo!

Dippy seemed relieved.

The splinter was as long as Jamie's arm, with a sharp point covered in mucus. Jamie tossed it into the undergrowth and then watched as Wanna nudged the soft ferns toward the huge dinosaur. Dippy gulped them down and raised its head.

Sluuurp! Sluurp! Sluurp!

A wet tongue the size of a bath towel, covered in spitty bits of fern and ginkgo goo, licked each of them in turn.

Sluuurp! Sluurp!

Sluurp!

"He's going to be OK!" Jamie and Tom leaped to their feet and shouted out in celebration. The vulture-like pterodactyls in the tree took off in alarm.

Dippy slowly clambered to its feet. Then it gently lowered its head and nuzzled first the boys, then Wanna, before turning and lumbering off into the forest.

"We did it!" Jamie grinned, wiping diplodocus drool off his face with the back of his hand. "We are dino dentists!"

They gave each other a high five. Ginkgo goop spattered down their bare arms.

"Help, Wanna!" Jamie and Tom shouted together, holding out their arms. They cringed as Wanna's sandpapery tongue rasped off every trace of ginkgo juice.

"It's probably time to go," Jamie said.

"But we haven't seen a dimorphodon," Tom said.

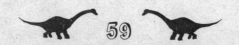

"We've used all the ginkgoes," Jamie reminded him, "so we can't bait any more birds."

"I suppose we've done enough 'bird' watching for one day," Tom agreed as they set off for Ginkgo Cave. "Archaeopteryx, rhamphorhynchus, and those horrible pterodactyls."

As they came to the clearing in front of the shallow cave, Jamie put his arm out to stop Tom. He put his finger to his lips.

"Look," he whispered. The ground was splattered with slimy, ripe ginkgoes. Waddling among them was a sand-colored creature, the size of a cat, with leathery wings and a long, spiky tail.

The boys watched as it sank its big red beak into the stinky fruit.

"Dimorphodon," Tom whispered. "My favorite flier."

The boys watched it for a moment until

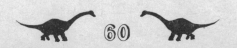

Wanna hurtled out of the jungle and the dimorphodon took off, flapping away over the treetops, honking as it flew. Wanna skidded to a halt and started to slurp up the ginkgoes.

Jamie smiled. "Wanna is terrible at bird-watching."

"He likes the bait too much," Tom replied. "See you next time, Wanna!"

The little dinosaur lifted his snout from the ginkgoes and wagged his tail as the boys stepped backward into the footprints. The ground turned to stone beneath their feet, and once more they were back in the secret chamber at the back of the Smugglers' Cave.

"Dino dentistry has made me hungry," Jamie said as they dashed to the lighthouse.

"Grandpa!" he called from the lighthouse door. "We're back! We're so hungry we could eat a dinosaur."

"Up here, me hearties," came the answering cry. The boys raced up the stairs to the kitchen.

Owwwww!

"I'll make some of my famous cheese and pickle sandwiches," the captain told them with a grin. "They'll only take a couple of minutes."

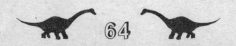

"I can't wait that long." Jamie spotted his grandfather's jar of homemade candy. He grabbed one and bit into it.

"Owwwww! My tooth!" he yelled.

"You're making more noise than a dinosaur at the dentist," Tom told him.

Jamie spluttered. "Not as much noise as someone swinging from the neck of a diplodocus."

"I wish I had your imaginations." Jamie's grandfather laughed as he cut up the sandwiches. "You sound as if you've had a fun day."

Jamie and Tom grinned at each other.

"We always have fun in Dinosaur Cove!"

GLOSSARY

Ammonite — an extinct animal with octopus-like legs, and often a spiral-shape shell, that lived in the ocean.

Archaeopteryx — the earliest bird capable of flight, with sharp teeth, three clawed fingers, and a long, bony tail. Archaeopteryx was not a fussy feeder, eating small animals, plants, and insects.

Dimorphodon — a flying reptile that had a long, pointed tail and big head with two different types of teeth.

Diplodocus — one of the longest land dinosaurs, with a long neck and whiplike tail. This huge dinosaur had pencil-shape blunt teeth perfect for its plant-only diet.

Ginkgo — a tree native to China called a "living fossil" because fossils of it have been found dating back millions of years, yet they are still around today. Also known as the stink bomb tree because of its smelly apricot-like fruit.

Jurassic — from about 150 to 200 million years ago, the Jurassic age was warm and humid, with lush jungle cover and great marine diversity. Large dinosaurs ruled on land, while the first birds took to the air.

Pterodactyl — a flying prehistoric reptile that could be as small as a bird or as large as an airplane.

Pterosaur — a prehistoric flying reptile. Its wings were leathery and light, and some of these "winged lizards" had fur on their bodies and bony crests on their heads.

Rhamphorhynchus — meat-eating flying reptile with a diamond-shape point of skin at the end of its long tail.

Wannanosaurus — a dinosaur that only ate plants and used its hard, flat skull to defend itself. Named after the place it was discovered: Wannano, in China.

YOU'D BETTER START RUNNING . . .
I'M COMING AFTER YOU!

Have you read all of Tom and Jamie's dino adventures?
If not, go back to the beginning!

Read all of Tom and Jamie's dinosaur adventures!